THE MOON

WATCHED IT ALL

SHELLEY A. LEEDAHL
& AINO ANTO

Red Deer Press

Published in Canada by Red Deer Press
195 Allstate Parkway, Markham, ON   L3R 4T8

Published in the United States by Red Deer Press
311 Washington Street, Brighton, MA   02135

Red Deer Press acknowledges with thanks the Canada Council for the Arts and the Ontario Arts Council for their support of our publishing program.
We acknowledge the financial support of the Government of Canada through the Canada Book Fund (CBF) for our publishing activities.

Library and Archives Canada Cataloguing in Publication
Leedahl, Shelley A. (Shelley Ann), 1963-, author
        The moon watched it all / Shelley A. Leedahl & Aino Anto.
ISBN 978-0-88995-537-0 (hardcover)
I. Anto, Aino, 1964-, illustrator II. Title.
PS8573.E3536M66 2019   jC813'.54   C2019-905769-6

Publisher Cataloging-in-Publication Data (U.S.)
Names: Leedahl, Shelley A. (Shelley Ann), 1963-, author. | Anto, Aino, illustrator.
Title: The Moon Watched All / Shelley A Leedahl & Aino Anto.
Description: Markham, Ontario : Red Deer Press, 2019. | Summary: An old woman spends her days in solitude with only the moon as witness. When she finds an orphan who has been rejected by his village, she invites him to stay with her and they create a new family.
 Identifiers: ISBN 978-0-88995-537-0 (hardcover)
 Subjects: LCSH: Loneliness -- Juvenile fiction. | Solitude -- Juvenile fiction. | Orphans -- Juvenile fiction. | BISAC: JUVENILE FICTION / Family / Alternative Family. | JUVENILE FICTION / Family / Orphans & Foster Homes.
Classification: LCC PZ7.L443Mo |DDC [F] – dc23

Edited for the Press by Peter Carver
Cover and interior design by Brooke Kerrigan
Printed in China by Scheck Wah Tong Printing

For Leah, Ashlynn, Reid, Annika,
Nash, James, Noah, Tate, and Sofie.
- S.A.L

For L.P.W. and M.W.W. as you each
put together your song.
- A.A

In a time before this time, when the world moved at a pony's pace, a woman rocked by her window and turned, every evening, to the moon.

"The hens are roosting and the village sleeps. It's you and me, Moon, together and alone. Tell me your news."

The woman was neither young nor old, neither happy nor particularly sad. She was known as Mirada, for she was always gazing. Like the moon, she was what she was.

Sometimes the moon responded to her query, but mostly it was just there, in the sky, being the moon.

At dawn, the sun jewelled tree and rooftops alike. Mirada stepped into the light and gathered brown eggs and vegetables, and the apples that hung gold as treasure-chest coins. She made a bucket with her apron, and when the weight of the harvest felt right, she climbed her stairs and took her bones to bed, remembering other apples, other mornings and seasons, and also, what could have been voices.

She closed the curtain and her room grew dim as a cave. She slept through the hours of the day, and though she longed to, she did not dream, ever.

Each night, after the sky had finished its fire dance and the sun reeled into the far-flung woods, Mirada awoke, made a pot of black tea, then took up her post and conversation.

"So here we are again, Moon, together and alone. My story is the same … my husband is gone, my children disappeared. You are my one true friend."

And so the nights stitched together into years.

Away from Mirada's house, the village transformed as the sun spooled up in the east. The baker was first awake, punching dough for bread that would sit like large round stones on the shelves, its fragrance drawing in the woman's neighbors, and the man who cobbled shoes, and also the boy with the great, dark eyes, who had no bread, nor any shoes, nor currency of any kind.

Did the child own even a name? No one knew. Boy, he was. Get Out Of The Way, Boy. And sometimes, Take That, Boy.

Like the woman with her moon was the boy with his sorrows. He passed his hours beside the pond in the great forest at the village edge, eating what the birds left after their fill of crusts and corn and seeds. Sometimes he fashioned sailboats from sticks and the maples' leaves. He ferried them along the water, singing a two-note song. Merry, merry, it went. Dream, dream. A fragment of a memory he could no longer keep in one piece.

The villagers paid scant attention. They had their commerce and their gossip and their feasts, and no moments left over for the woman who avoided the day, no time for the tongue-locked boy.

Except sometimes. Sometimes children thundered after the boy and he'd scramble into the almost-impossible trees. He was nimble, and quick to hide from their taunts and stones.

So quiet. So forever he could hold his breath, his sun-browned skin disappearing against tree limbs. Occasionally, beneath the breeze, he made the sounds that were his one little song: Merry, merry. Row, boat. And the children believed it a trick of the wind.

Beneath quarter moons, the halves, and the barely-theres. The moon-pies without a single slice missing. Through rainstorm, and wind whorls, dry summer-bakes, and the long white sleds of January. Through and beneath, alongside and over, the boy grew into and out of the rags folks had left on their clotheslines, and he made discoveries, as boys will, even when hunger thrums against their ribs.

There was nothing for him in the village, and thus he walked its lanes less and less. Only the vast forest embraced him. He scooped the earth, and lay where it was cool, the small creatures accepting him as their own. He built forts among the tangled woods and bush berries, and moved at will between them. He swam between cattails, slicing the moon's reflection upon the coppered water.

Then he peered up through the lace of leaves from his grassy bed, and thought no further than morning. Like the large-eyed animals that sipped from the pond, he kept far from human sight.

In her wood-neighboring house, the woman rocked and held ever more conversations with the moon. "O wondrous ear," she crooned. "O great goose eye."

She praised it, like she once prized her children, in a time before a time that was then.

"You are such a wise moon. Such a handsome moon. A round book of secrets. You direct tides and rule the starry galleria."

Her blood was a river merging with sea; her hand fluttered near her heart, like a wing.

Light, the moon sometimes said. Sleeper. Maybe good.

"Riddles and rhymes," Mirada mused, unbothered. "These are the moon's own way." She picked her way through the puzzling language, no greater chore than sorting ripe raspberries from green, good radishes from those gone to worms.

There came a day harder than all the others. The boy knelt to drink from the pond-water, and was met there by a man with crushing boots, nothing more than dirt in his mouth.

Get you, Boy.

The stranger grabbed, and the rags on the boy's back fell apart in the terrible fingers. Logs, and puddles, and the chasing man. Rocks, and roots, and clawing hands.

The boy ran until dizzy, until dry. West of the pond, away from trees he knew like brothers. Until his feet were raw. His chest aflame. And he could run no more.

When it was safe to look back, the sun had dropped behind the dark smudge of the now distant woods, and the wicked man was gone, like smoke. But the boy was gone now, too. Lost. He collapsed into a hollow among the tall yellow grass, and the larks sang, and frogs chirruped, keeping a kind of time with the crickets that were like shiny black buttons on the clothes he'd never worn.

Night came calling, and he thought of boots, of heels, and the finger-quick hands. He thought of the children with sticks, and villagers who possessed the power to look right through him. The boy held out his own hand, and could not keep it steady.

A nighthawk announced itself with an echoing peep. A cloud shifted across the stars. The boy flinched. He was afraid of it all now, of everything that moved or breathed — and the moon.

He struggled against sleep, but it won for a time. When he opened his eyes, night was still there. And a sound, in the distance … a bird and not a bird. Only hunger compelled him to follow and find it.

Carefully, back through the dark the way he thought he had fled, between the woods and the pond, over the frail, snapping branches and age-worn stones. Where were his feet taking him?

— To the village …

— But he couldn't …

— Yet his hunger …

— The man in the boots …

— To the village … and in.

The sound, closer now. And then a wire fence, a gate off its hinges. He pushed inside, crossed a garden, and further, where the bird sounds had almost settled, he entered a coop and collapsed for a time among the feathers.

The moon moved a few inches to the right, and the boy awoke. He stepped into the nearly-straight-growing rows. Carrots. Potatoes. Peas he skinned with broken fingernails and poured into the cave of his mouth.

Then: he slept almost as well as any other boy.

At the window, the moon had a message for the woman.

Boy, it said. Garden.

Feet go.

But Mirada was enjoying her rocking, her warming tea. Her face in the moon's unwavering spotlight. She was a lake unruffled, the coal fire's glow. And she ignored the moon's declaration.

The boy rose with the sun. He dusted the soil from his face. Where was he? A garden. Ah, yes. Yesterday was the park. The crushing boots and the lurching man wearing them.

He felt his stomach. Last night, he'd eaten. What now? Not far away, fruit-sellers, calling in the market. A woman screaming at her daughters. There were dogs out there, beyond the broken-down gate, and machines with too many teeth. The children who mocked. What was the why-for of it? Day was to be feared, the boy decided, but his belly was making all decisions now. He crept among the raspberry scratch-bushes and scramble-climbed the apple tree. He snuck into the coop with the fidgeting chickens. And when he spied a woman on the steps, he made himself flat as a hide, quiet as a pine cone among the garden's leafy plants.

And it was fine.

Night's shadow fell again, and at
her window with the moon, Mirada
sensed movement in her garden. The shape
of something. She stood, and her chair
continued rocking without her.

"Moon, we may have company tonight."

Was it a dog? A deer? The shadow changed.
Two legs, not four. A boy, it was. And walking-stick thin.

"This is surely a mystery, Moon. But I have you and you
have me. We are enough for each other."

Her own words offered no reassurance.

"Tired. Night," she said. "I am beginning to speak like you,
Moon. Perhaps I am becoming moon. Maybe this is how it happens."

The moon was quiet, and because she had listened extra hard, and
rocked at double speed, when the hours added up and the sun glazed the
rooftops, Mirada was too tired to gather vegetables or eggs. She crawled
into the soft bed behind her curtain, and did not sleep, her legs moving as
if she were running—from what? From whom?

Night fell into the deeps. The boy left his shelter among the nearly-straight rows, and crept again toward the shed. The garden's goodness, and now one brown-speckled egg, warm as light. He measured it against the moon. How easy it had been. He opened the single egg, and drank, then cupped his hands in the barrel's rainwater, as close to happy as he'd ever been.

Merrily, a faded voice. The stream.

Mirada again took up her window-side perch.

"Good evening, mister Moon. Anything to tell me tonight?"

For many moments the moon was silent, and the woman rocked. She listened harder than she ever had before. She surveyed the stars for activity. Unsettled, she keened toward the moon, lest she miss a solitary word.

Help, came the voice, sounding, like always, as if it were coming from within herself. You.

Outside, a shape. The shadow again, and now it was growing into a boy. Looking at her. Mirada's hands trembled, like birds born to snow.

She wanted to remember things. Her children. How she'd cared for them. How they had brought her little gifts — posies, and feathers. Kind words. They raced through the woods and swung from wonderland-trees, falling into cushion-heaped leaves.

Look at me. Over here. See what I can do, Mama.

Her heart made its own kind of sound.

Moon watched, and listened.

The child stood in the starlight. He stared back at the figure in the window, and like the words that sometimes occurred to him, he remembered a woman, and how he crept into her lap, and every so often, when her hand combed his hair, her voice met his ear. That little singing.

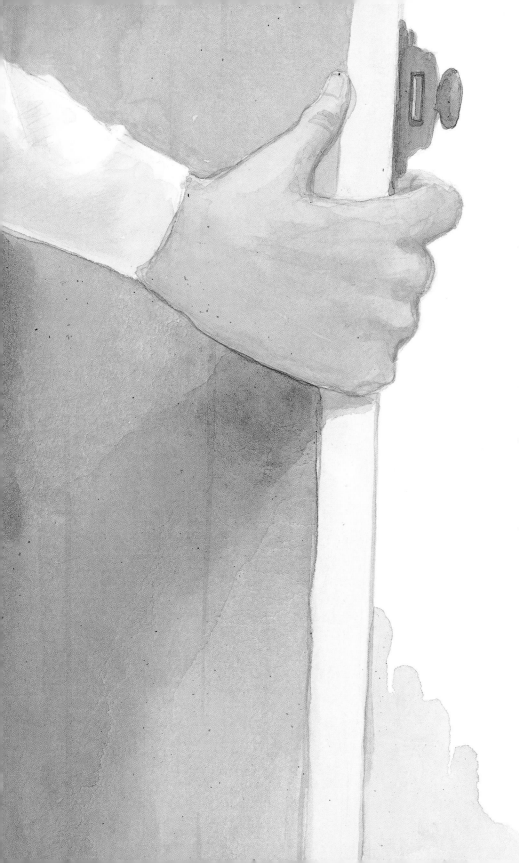

"Moon?" The woman was waiting.

You know, Moon said. You are.

Mirada rose. In each step she felt all the years that had passed since she'd stopped counting time.

"Boy," she said. And then again: "Boy."

He came, slowly, knowing this as his name.

Tea in the pot, garden soup, bread. She fed the child, the moon or some time before this time telling her this was how it must begin. When he had filled himself, she made a bed on the floor by the fire, and returned to her rocking-without-her chair.

The moon polished the boy. He was like a cat, small and tucked into himself. Mirada ached to be told how, what next, but the moon had nothing to say. And the boy-child was ever-fast dreaming.

The rain in the barrel spilled over and over, and hummingbirds drank from the delphiniums. Time followed with an order that neither Mirada nor the boy seemed to set.

The first morning he found an axe in the shed and returned to the woods. When she woke to the chopping, Mirada saw that he had piled one tall stack, and a second was already growing.

She would sleep, and he would wake. Potatoes washed and peeled. The floor swept. He held up a pot, and saw himself. He scrubbed at the washtub until his skin stung. Mirada rummaged in her closet and mined out two shirts, and pants the boy belted with rope. Sometimes he just sat on the floor beside the fire, waiting for what would happen. But nothing happened quickly — the world moved at a slower pace then.

After several more nights, their rhythms began overlapping, like clouds tossed by a spirited wind. The boy made the fires and Mirada set her hands to deep-dish pies rich with raspberries and apples. They ate at the table together, and when the sun disappeared behind the trees, the woman drew another chair to the window, and the pair sat almost like friends beneath the moon.

Mirada rocked and hummed and sipped her strong black tea, and the boy made a sound that was not singing and was not humming, but it was something. Each night he stayed up a few minutes later and she shuffled to bed a few moments earlier, so that in time — in a great deal of time — their days and nights matched, and she spoke less to the know-everything moon and more to the boy, who, like the moon, did not talk much, but kept her company just the same.

The village people saw them together in the market.

Is that the woman who talks to the moon?

Is that Get Away From Here, Boy?

Eventually time did its work, and the villagers became accustomed to seeing them. The taunting children became mothers and fathers with more to concern themselves with than a boy who had become a man and still had no name.

In the meantime, the apple tree yielded. Shoes were bought once, and again. There were more chickens, a goat, then two cows. The moon watched it all.

And the woman named for her gazing sometimes smiled, sometimes dreamed. And the boy put together his song.